Dedication

This is book is dedicated to:

All of Pepe's loyal supporters and friends, near and far, who have welcomed Pepe into their hearts and lovingly shared his adventures. Thank you for being part of his journey and always inspiring him to seek out new discoveries.

For all those who love adventure and love to discover new things:
May you find many new, glorious discoveries!

Acknowledgements

I'd like to thank the wonderful staff at L'Auberge de Sedona who kindly and generously allowed me access to their gorgeous property that inspired the backdrop setting for this book. It was a delight to share Pepe's experience of this very special location.

I am also deeply grateful to Kate Roberge, of Kate's Books in Jerome, Arizona, long-time client and friend. Her keen editorial eye always spots the inevitable things I miss. Thank you for your patience in being my sounding board for the numerous, creative braining-storming sessions I've subjected you to as I've worked through my plot points and for being one of Pepe's greatest champions. Your gracious and invaluable insights always help me create the very best adventures possible for my readers!

**Other Books in the Adventures of PEPE QUACKAMOLE™ series
(also available on Kindle)**
by Rita M. Reger

A Duck in the Desert

Pepe Quacks the Case of the Wailing Miner

A Duck in the Caboose

**For additional information:
www.pepequackamole.com**

Rita M. Reger
Integrity Path Ventures, LLC
PO. Box 20671
Sedona, AZ 86341

www.facebook.com/rita.m.reger

A Duck by the Creek

A PEPE QUACKAMOLE™ Adventure

Written, Illustrated and Published by

Rita M. Reger

Best Wishes.

Rita M. Reger

Could they be here yet? Pepe wondered. A bright yellow wing tightly clutched his suitcase. The little yellow duck in the sombrero and colored scarf shifted from one duck foot to the other and back again, as he waited his turn at the hotel's front desk.

"Checking in?" asked the kind lady with the even kinder eyes. Finally, it was his turn! He flew up and peered over the edge of the hotel desk, barely reaching his bright orange beak over the top. The desk was so high, he had to stand on a stack of suitcases so he could see.

"Hello! My name is Pepe Quackamole. I am meeting my family here. Can you tell me if the Johnsons from Chicago are here yet?"

Any minute now, he would be close to his family after a long time apart. What a grand adventure this will be! It was going to be great to reconnect with his human family, but more importantly, with his little boy, Billy. It seemed so long ago since they'd all come on vacation together. Pepe had accidently been left behind in the desert on that trip. He'd had so many wonderful adventures and made so many new friends in his new adopted home, now he didn't even mind that he'd gotten lost! But he'd sure missed Billy a lot, so it would be great to see him again.

Pepe had been so excited to get Billy's letter saying they were coming for a visit and were staying at L'Auberge de Sedona, a beautiful resort hotel right on the edge of Oak Creek in Sedona, Arizona. Sitting by the creek and catching up with his buddy about all their favorite things sounded like a great way to spend a few relaxing days. He couldn't wait to tell Billy about the fun adventures he'd had and hear all about Billy's news, too.

The lady returned with his key and some other information about his stay at the hotel. When she'd explained everything, she said, "The Johnsons checked in just a little while ago. Mrs. Johnson has an appointment at the spa later this afternoon, so maybe you can meet up with her there. Someone just saw Mr. Johnson and his son head down towards the creek. You can leave your suitcase with us if you want to try to catch up with them. It would be our pleasure to put it in your room for you."

He gave her a thankful "Quack!" and waddled quickly out the door to find Billy.

Dear Pepe,

Guess what?!   We are coming to visit you in Sedona!

Your stories of the southwest sounded so wonderful, we just had to come see it for ourselves.   Mom, Dad and I will be staying at a beautiful hotel, right on Oak Creek, called L'Auberge de Sedona. Pack your suitcase and come relax with us by the creek for a few days!

Can't wait to catch up with you and learn more about the beautiful new place you've discovered!

Love,
Billy

As soon as he walked through the terrace doors, Pepe stopped in his webbed tracks. He couldn't believe what he saw. Everywhere he looked there were large, white sycamore trees that seemed to go up, up and up with leaves disappearing into the sky. In front of him was a large patio area with tables and chairs, but the grandest thing of all was a beautiful creek with rocks. He inhaled deeply and got a large beakful of wonderful nature smells. But there was another tasty smell coming from the restaurant, too. He would have to come back later and see what yummy things waited for him.

The tables and chairs were all nestled quietly between the trees along the edge of the creek. Oh, he couldn't wait to share this with his human family! He hurried down a set of stone steps and came to a wooden foot bridge. He stopped on the bridge for a minute to watch the water dance across the rocks. Splish! Splash! Gurgle! Bubble! Splish! The water looked like it was having a great time, bouncing across the rocks in the creek.

Just beyond the leaves, he heard a familiar sound. "Quack! Quack!" Was that a... duck?! Running over the bridge and across a sandy area as quickly as a waddling duck can run, he came to a row of white, wooden lounge chairs that sat all along the edge of the water. When he looked into the water, he saw a group of pretty ducks splashing around. They weren't yellow like him, but green and brown and some even had deep blue stripes on their wings. "Quack!" they all said together. But in duck language, Pepe heard "Welcome" and was glad. What friendly ducks they were!

"Hello! What is this place?" Pepe asked them.

A large duck with a beautiful green head swam up. "We call it 'Duck Beach.' My name is Francis. We live here in Oak Creek."

"Oak Creek?!" Pepe recognized that name. "Why, I've swum in Oak Creek before, just in a different part of it. I had no idea it came all the way over here."

The duck named Francis continued, "We like this part the best. We think it's one of the prettiest areas, so we spend a lot of time here. It's usually quiet and peaceful. The guests that stay at the resort feed us breakfast every morning. We love it here. What brings you to our resort?"

"My human family is visiting Sedona and I've come to meet them. I've been traveling here in the southwest and haven't seen them in quite a while," Pepe explained. "I'm Pepe Quackamole! Pleased to meet you," Pepe said, extending a yellow wing to shake Francis' brown one. "Say, you haven't seen a red-haired little boy with freckles, have you?"

"Why yes, actually, we have," Francis answered. "In fact, he was just here with his dad. They fed us some duck snacks and took pictures. I heard him saying he wished his duck was here to see this. I guess he must've been talking about you. I think they said they were going to see the salt water pool next."

"Thank you so much for the information. I should get going and see if I can find them. I'm so excited to see them again but haven't been able to find them yet. I'm sure they're here at the resort somewhere! It was so nice to meet you."

"You too, Pepe. Please come back and swim with us, anytime – we will show you all the beautiful spaces along the creek that only ducks and other creek creatures can find." Now *that* sounded like it would be a lot of fun, Pepe thought, as he waved goodbye to his new friends.

What lucky ducks they were to be able to live in such a beautiful place!

Pepe followed the signs for the pool and pushed open a big gate once he reached it. When he got inside, he saw a large swimming pool. Pepe had never been in a salt water pool before. Pepe loved to try new things, especially if it involved water. He thought of his friend, Fred, who probably would not have been so excited about the salt water pool. You see, Fred was a frog and one of Pepe's very best friends, but Fred was very shy around water, so Pepe didn't push him to get in if he wasn't quite ready. That was just fine with Pepe – they'd had so many other wonderful adventures together outside of the water that he didn't mind at all that Fred didn't want to swim.

Pepe took off his sombrero and scarf and laid them on a nearby chair. The pool attendant had swim goggles for Pepe to wear so he put them on his bright yellow head and splashed into the pool, flapping loudly and happily. He quacked and splashed and quacked some more. He was enjoying himself so much, he'd almost forgotten to look for Billy! Yikes! He really should continue his search. But where should he go next?

His tummy made a loud growl. Good idea, tummy, thought Pepe, patting his yellow belly. All that swimming had made him hungry. Maybe Billy had gotten hungry, too, and was eating at the restaurant. Yes, that sounded like a good plan. He'd check the restaurant next and grab a quick bite to eat.

When Pepe arrived at the restaurant, he still didn't see Billy. Not at a table, not in a chair, and not near the creek. He let out a big sigh. Will I ever find Billy? he wondered, his wings drooping. Where could he be? He'd just have to keep looking. But first, he needed to eat!

Pepe sat down at a lovely little table, right on the edge of the water. The server came by with a glass of water and a menu. Pepe looked over the menu and tried to pick just one thing – it was hard to pick just one, it all looked so delicious. And the desserts! Oh, my goodness! He would definitely have to tell Fred about the desserts! If Fred saw all those yummy choices, he might just be willing to sit by the water, after all! Fred loved desserts. After placing his order, Pepe watched the creek flow right by and could see Francis and the other ducks swimming further away. It was fun to watch the sunlight play peek-a-boo through the leaves of the trees and then shine down on the creek. Sometimes it would bounce around on top of the water, making a brilliant sparkle as the sun met with the water. It almost looked like the sun was dancing or playing hopscotch on the creek! That made Pepe smile. In the background, he heard the clink of glasses and dishes as staff and servers moved around quickly, carefully balancing large trays of food. Soon his meal would be here, too.

The wind soared suddenly, making a loud *whoosh!* noise as it rustled through the leaves, fluffed up Pepe's face feathers and then drifted away again. It felt good on a hot, summer day to feel the wind dry his feathers from his swim in the pool. When his meal arrived, he savored each mouthful and asked the server, "Excuse me? What time is it?" He found out that it was five minutes before Mrs. Johnson's spa appointment. Oh, no! He'd been enjoying his meal and the creek so much, he'd forgotten all about the time again! He had to get to get going if he was going to meet up with her in time!

As he walked through the grounds, he saw small, log cabins around every corner. It looked like a small village tucked into the trees. Each building had a porch, lounge chairs, and seating areas that were perfect for relaxing amidst the nature sounds and watching the creek. He could still see his new duck friends swimming back and forth in the distance. Occasionally, one of them would dive under the water and then pop up with a sudden spray of water. It made him giggle.

As he walked further into the property, the sound of the creek and the ducks became softer and softer until he could hardly hear them. At the center of the property, he saw large outdoor sculptures, a small pond and lots of pretty trees, flowers and bushes. Stone walking paths wound their way between the cabins and the trees and all the other buildings.

Pepe followed one of the stone paths to the spa, but it wasn't soon enough. They told him Mrs. Johnson had just gone in for her appointment and it would be a long time before she was done. The woman at the spa desk asked, "Would you like to have a treatment while you wait for her? We have many relaxing options to choose from." Pepe bobbed his yellow head up and down.

They gave him a thick, cuddly spa robe to wear and a glass of cucumber and orange water to drink while he waited. How refreshing that was. Pepe had never had cucumber and orange water before, but he sure liked it! He sat in the waiting area, next to a cozy fireplace with soft music playing. He closed his eyes and relaxed so much during his massage, he even fell asleep for a few minutes at the end! By the time he came back out, Mrs. Johnson had already left, again! Well, there was only one place left to check. They all had to be back at the room, by now. He'd go there next.

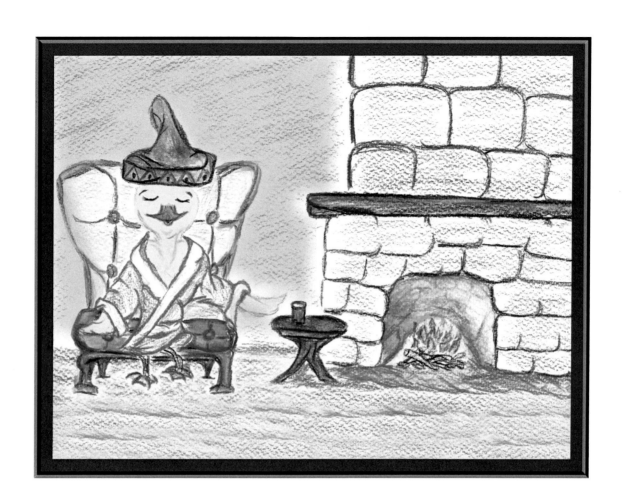

Pepe arrived at the room and found the door cracked open. He pushed it open carefully with his wing and called, "Hello?" He heard no response. He walked through the door and quacked it a little louder "Helloooo!" Still nothing. Several suitcases sat on the floor. They must be here, somewhere. The room had a beautiful bed, a fireplace and a patio in the front. He walked out on the patio. They weren't there either, but he could hear the wind *Swish!* and the soft gurgling of Oak Creek in the distance. Hmmm, maybe they are out back. He opened a door at the back of the suite and found an outdoor shower. How neat was that?! He would definitely need to try that out later. But still, no family.

Stumped, he came back in the room and sat on the bed to think. Rubbing his beak, he thought and thought, but still couldn't figure out where they might be. The bed underneath him was so soft he thought he might just lie down for a minute and rest his eyes. He had gotten pretty tired from the swim, all that great food, and the massage. Before he knew it, he started to dream of floating down the creek with his duck friends. Little duck snores, escaped from his beak. *Quack! Snort! Quack!* In his dream, Pepe heard the rustling of leaves and the gently flowing creek. The sun warmed his feathers as he floated among the other ducks, rocks and trees. After a few minutes, Pepe's dreams of floating on the creek were interrupted by a loud clicking noise. Could that be the sound of a branch breaking along the creek? Was it all still part of his dream?

What he heard next was no dream. "There he is! We've finally found him!" a small voice squealed with delight. Pepe recognized that voice! It was Billy! Popping his eyes open wide just to make sure he wasn't dreaming, Pepe saw nothing but freckles and a bunch of curly red hair staring at him, eyeball-to-eyeball. Billy, his little human boy hugged him tight and squeezed the breath right out of him. "I've been looking all over for you!" Billy hugged Pepe even tighter as Pepe gave a little SQUEAK!

Pepe giggled. The whole time he'd been looking for Billy, Billy had been looking for him, too. They probably had gone round and round the resort following each other and not even knowing it! Pepe and Billy both thought that was funny. Mr. and Mrs. Johnson smiled at them, happy to see Pepe, too.

"Oh, it's so good to see you!" Billy said. "I can't wait to you tell you everything I've done while you've been away!" Pepe couldn't wait, either. He thought he had just the perfect place to catch up. He even had some new friends for Billy to meet, too.

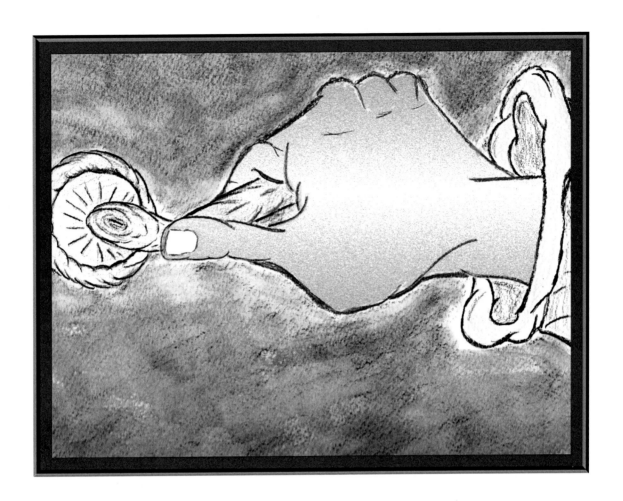

On the way down to the creek, Billy talked non-stop about all the things he had been doing. Relaxing in a lounge chair on the banks of Oak Creek, Pepe watched the ducks give a little wave as they swam past. In the blowing breeze, Pepe smiled, too, as he waved at Francis floating by in the creek in front of him, looking forward to swimming with them soon.

As Billy talked and talked, Pepe closed his eyes, happy to be spending time with his friend again. He couldn't think of a better place to be and a better sound to hear than the gurgle of the creek, the whisper of the wind and the happy voice of Billy telling him all about *his* adventures. His little duck heart was full.

He was a happy duck, indeed!

The End

Explore More! Who, What, Where?

Note: Unless other sources are specifically cited, information in this section represents the author's general understanding, in the author's own words, and is included only to help provide context to potentially new concepts or locations introduced in the story. Where available, original source links have been included.

Where is Sedona, Arizona?

Sedona, Arizona is located in the north central area of Arizona and is known for its dramatic red rock landscape and as a hiking and outdoor recreation area.

What kinds of fun things can you do in Sedona, Arizona?

Sedona gets millions of visitors every year that enjoy hiking, camping, enjoying the beautiful views of Sedona's famous red rocks, taking fun and exciting tours, learning about history, relaxing by the creek, stargazing in a dark sky, exploring beautiful art galleries and shops, and so much more! Find about all the great places you can go and fun things you can do in Sedona at:

https://visitsedona.com/

Where is the place that Pepe visited with his family?

Pepe and his family visited L'Auberge de Sedona, a hotel resort located in Sedona, Arizona:

www.lauberge.com

What is Oak Creek?

Oak Creek is a waterway that winds its way through the Sedona, Arizona area. It begins in the north at the top of Oak Creek canyon, connecting to the Verde River in the south. Oak Creek helped carve the shape of today's Oak Creek Canyon over 8 million years ago. The creek travels across about 300,000 acres and provides lots of places to go hiking, camping and enjoying the pretty views of the outdoors along the creek. Several parts of it are included in federally designated wilderness areas and state parks. Groups exist that help protect it for everyone to enjoy. Find out more about the creek at:

https://oakcreekwatershed.org/
https://oakcreekwatershed.org/oak-creek-visitors/recreational-opportunites

What kind of duck is Francis?

Francis and most of his duck friends that live in Oak Creek are mallards. There are many different kinds of mallards and some look very different from the others. Find out more about mallards at:

https://en.wikipedia.org/wiki/Mallard

Can ducks live in salt water?

Yes! Ducks can live in both salt water or freshwater, as Pepe discovers in this story, when he experiences a salt water pool for the first time! Find out more about the differences between salt water found in oceans and freshwater at:

https://sciencing.com/four-between-ocean-fresh-water-8519973.html

For Additional Explore More! Information, visit:
www.pepequackamole.com

Made in the USA
San Bernardino, CA
05 August 2019